The Cursed Princess

Shiva Kumar

pencil

ISBN 978-93-5610-986-5
© Shiva Kumar 2022
Published in India 2022 by Pencil

A brand of
One Point Six Technologies Pvt. Ltd.
123, Building J2, Shram Seva Premises,
Wadala Truck Terminal, Wadala (E)
Mumbai 400037, Maharashtra, INDIA
E connect@thepencilapp.com
W www.thepencilapp.com

Author biography

Hi, my name is Shiva. This is my first book

CONTENTS

Chapter-1 The Beginning

It was a village of modest means, houses made of wood and rooves of thatch, and primarily making its income from logging. The town's forest was old and home to some of the tallest trees in the land. When princess Nioli had time off from tutoring, she would stare into the forest's dark with an ever-burning curiosity. On some days, it seemed as if the trees bent over the tall stone wall that encircled the village as if trying to reclaim the small plot of land the town occupied. On a day when her tutors had let her off early, she decided she would walk to the edge, right to the gray stone wall that stood between her and the forest and see if she could cross. Her father forbade her from entering the woods even on the brightest day and with an armed guard. Today though, wrapped in a dark blue cloak and a pack slung over one shoulder, she would cross over the wall or through the gates to the forest beyond. No one noticed the cloaked figure as they sped down the castle's steps and through the village, busy with trade and work. She reached the stone wall in a heap of excited nerves, quickly stepping back into the shadow of a nearby house to observe the wall before her. There were guards atop it and patrols every so often below. There were two gates, the closest being only a hundred paces to her left. She had to decide the most accessible and least conspicuous way to escape to the forest beyond--at least for just this afternoon. The princess stared up at the wall again, then looked around and caught sight of a path leading away from the wall, towards one of the many paths that wound out of the village and into the woods. That would be safer than jumping across it. Nioli slipped behind the cover of a nearby shrub and peered through the foliage to watch the path. When nothing happened, she darted forward, keeping low and close to the ground to avoid making noise as her bare feet slapped against the hard earth. A twig snapped underfoot as she passed beneath one of the more enormous gates, and she froze instantly. "What?" she whispered, hoping no one was within earshot. The gate swung shut, and she heard footfalls approaching from another direction. Nioli spun around to find several men bearing spears coming in her order. One of them shouted for everyone to hold their positions. The others hurried past the startled princess without sparing her a glance, heading down the road leading away from the gate and toward the forest. Forcing herself to relax and slow her breathing, Nioli watched until they disappeared from sight. She then crept forward on her toes to peer around the next corner. Nothing moved on the other side. Taking a deep breath, she stepped onto the path again and continued strolling, listening for movement. After she had gone three dozen paces, the course ended abruptly on top of a short cliff, offering her a fantastic view of the village that spread below her. To her left was a wide river, sparkling in the late spring sunshine, and on her right was a field full of colorful flowers that glittered like tiny jewels in the sunlight. A clear, calm stream flowed swiftly out of sight at her feet. In front of the bridge, a group of children played on the grass, tossing sticks into the water, while some adults sat under trees to rest. As if reading her thoughts, a pair of birds flew overhead, swooping down to pick up the fallen stick and return it to the air. Nioli took a moment to absorb the beauty around her. This must have been the first time since her parents' death that she had felt peace. For a split second, she wondered whether it might really come true and that someday there could be no more pain, no more tears or worries, no more fear of falling. It might never happen, of course; the thought brought her little comfort. But if it ever did… Her mother's voice echoed inside her head, bringing her back to the present. "If you wish to live like a princess, Nioli, remember your heritage. You must know that you can do nothing wrong unless you act according to our traditions. We are still here to guide you, but now I must leave you. Your father has business to attend to in the city, and I must oversee everything." Nioli closed her eyes and tried to force the memory away. Still, it remained, a constant reminder that her life might yet change forever. And that her fate, whether bad or good, could very well depend upon which she chose to believe. "Well, it looks like my job here is finished." Startled, Nioli whirled around to see a young woman overseeing her at the end of the pathway. She was dressed in a long black dress, covered from ankle to mid-knee in intricate designs and embroidery in various shades of red, blue, green, purple, and yellow. Around her neck hung an intricately decorated silver chain that seemed to glow like fire. Long blonde hair fell loose from her braid, framing delicate features of pale, perfect porcelain skin. In the bright sunlight of the clearing, she sparkled brilliantly like a star. As Nioli took in all these details, the woman smiled. "It appears that you may not have seen me arrive."

Nioli shook her head. "Sorry, my eyes were fixed on something else." The woman nodded. "That makes sense. Do forgive me if I intruded; I didn't mean to interrupt. My name is Frelia." She bowed slightly. "I am pleased to make your acquaintance." "My pleasure to meet you too. My name is Nioli. What brings you here?" "Ah, well…" Frelia blushed slightly. "This is an adventure in the forest and one I am told you might appreciate. If you will follow me…." Frelia turned toward a thicket near the side of the trail. Without waiting for a response, she began to hurry through the brush, frequently pausing to allow Nioli to catch up. Nioli stumbled, tripping over roots or bushes that were too dense to get past, but soon recovered and kept pace behind Frelia as the woman continued moving deeper and deeper into the forest. Eventually, they stopped in the shadow of a large tree, far enough back to be hidden from most people yet close enough to hear them calling out to one another from afar. "Do take a seat, Miss…?" "Just Nioli." Frelia offered her a smile. "Thank you. I hope this doesn't offend you. My husband and I prefer to stay together, and separating during the winter is difficult. I usually travel by myself, but it gets lonely. So, if you don't mind spending a few hours alone with me, we could try something different today. Maybe we can talk. Would that be alright with you, Miss…?" "Oh, I suppose that wouldn't hurt anything." Nioli sighed with relief and plopped down onto the forest floor, grateful for the shade the tree provided. "What do you suggest we talk about?" "I have been curious about you since the beginning," she replied. "There's something about you familiar like I should have met you, but I simply cannot recall. Is it because I've seen you before?" Nioli chuckled. "Maybe it is. But that's silly, isn't it? Who doesn't recognize Princess Nioli?" "No matter how hard I think on it, I can't seem to place the resemblance. Perhaps we can discuss that later, after we've talked a bit longer, hmm? Now, where were we? Ah, yes, about you...." They spent hours talking and joking around, talking about their families, homes, and friends while Frelia explained her role as a servant of the King and his queen. Nioli shared stories about her childhood adventures and her dreams of being a knight and traveling to faraway lands like those in the books her tutor once read to her. It was nice to finally have someone to share all her thoughts and feelings with who didn't already know who she was. After a while, Frelia started to yawn and asked if she could go to sleep. "Of course!" Nioli exclaimed, feeling guilty when she realized how long they had spent talking. She gathered the small pouch containing the golden apple into her hands, tucking it safely away under her sleeve. "Are you certain you won't stay for supper?" Frelia hesitated, then shook her head. "No, thank you. I'm afraid I'm too tired to sit at the table with the others tonight. Tomorrow, maybe, if you would like?" "Yes, tomorrow sounds fine. Thank you for joining us." She grinned sheepishly. "But we can probably wait another day or two." Frelia smiled. "Goodnight, Nioli." She waited until she could no longer hear the soft footsteps of the woman as she retreated through the woods, then turned quickly and began retracing her steps back the way she had come. When she reached the gate, she glanced over her shoulder just in time to watch as a dark shape emerged from the shadows of the path behind her and vanished into the darkness beyond. She smiled to herself in satisfaction. That should keep him busy for a while. "Come along," she said softly. "Let's see what mischief he's gotten himself into this time." Nioli climbed onto the horse's back and slid her legs onto its sides. She tightened the leather girth and looked down at Ryn. "Ready for another adventure?" With a quick kick from her heels, the horse jumped forward, racing across the clearing, sending leaves flying and scattering branches in every direction. Nioli clung to the saddle as the animal leaped high, almost throwing her off into the dirt. A few moments later, the horse slowed down and settled into a trot, then picked up speed again as it headed back toward camp. The sun shone brightly above, making the ground sparkle like diamonds. Nioli gazed ahead, taking in all the sights and smells of her new home. There was the smell of freshly baked bread wafting out of the cookpot on the back porch of their temporary house. Another scent came drifting from the kitchen window, sweet, enticing, and tempting, and Nioli found herself inhaling deeply. Suddenly, she felt a light pressure against her arm, and looking down, she saw her dog leaning against her leg. "Hey, Rosie, look," she said, nudging the dog. "We're almost home. Can you taste it already? Just think of it. We'll be eating dinner soon…." She laughed to herself. "You have to admit it does sound nice to say that." Suddenly, a loud thump sounded from nearby, followed by a yelp. Startled, Nioli looked over in time to see Frelia fall from the tree and hit the ground with a loud crash. Rosie barked excitedly, dancing circles around the lost girl, wagging his tail furiously. Nioli gasped. Oh, dear... Frelia groaned and sat up. "Ow….that really hurt. That was a nasty fall." She winced when she looked up and noticed that Nioli was staring at her intently. Blushing slightly, she waved awkwardly. "Hello? Are you still there?" A small smile formed on her face as she nodded. "Yeah, sorry. It was just… wow, it seems like you could have broken some bones or knocked yourself unconscious. You alright?" Frelia rubbed her head. "Yeah, everything hurts now that I mention it…." "Do you need help up?" "Um, sure." Nioli hopped off her horse and helped the princess back to her feet. "I'll have Rosie take you to the healers, and they'll give you something to make you feel better." She looked at the princess questioningly. "Do you want us to walk there together?" Frelia shook her head. "No, that's alright. You enjoy your evening, miss Nioli. Don't worry, I'm fine now. I promise." Nioli nodded and gave her a smile. "Alright. See you tomorrow morning." With that, she hurried off toward her parents' house, leaving Frelia standing there. She watched the young woman running toward the trees with a confused expression. For some reason, she wasn't comfortable letting Nioli walk alone in the dark forest, even if she couldn't remember ever seeing her . She hoped the girl would find her way back to camp safely and be returned to her parents without further incident, for if Frelia didn't return with her, it would indeed cause quite a stir. And if word got back to her father, he wouldn't hesitate to punish the entire village if anything untoward happened. Not only that, but he would also undoubtedly suspect that she had been responsible. He was very suspicious of everyone; it was why he hired Nioli's mother to help with their cooking. As Frelia wandered farther into the darkness, she tried to put it from her mind and focus instead on finding an opening in the foliage, hoping to reach another part of Faerun without encountering any trouble. The night grew colder, and she pulled her cloak tighter around herself. She wondered why she always seemed lost in these woods and whether the strange occurrences here had anything to do with that. Whatever they were, they weren't friendly. She shuddered, not liking the idea of meeting up with the mysterious stranger again. No doubt her father would be furious if she managed to stumble upon them again… Suddenly, she heard a rustling in the bushes and spun around in alarm. The moonlight illuminated something moving in the dark, but she didn't have time to ponder what it could be as a loud growl erupted from within the trees, and she heard the sound of fangs snapping at the air. "RUN!" The scream was ripped straight from Nioli's throat, and she dashed away from the bushes and sprinted through the forest, desperately trying to get away from the predator. Her heart pounded loudly in her chest as she ran, her breath coming in short bursts, and tears threatened to fall from her eyes as the Beast's footsteps approached from behind. Please let me live, please let me live, please let me-- She tripped over a large root, falling onto her knees in a heap of tangled limbs. She struggled to stand, but a strong, clawed hand grabbed her and lifted her from the ground, slamming her against a thick trunk. The creature growled menacingly, baring its teeth like a wild animal searching for flesh. The moon reflected off of its sharp eyes and gleamed off of long, spiky fur. Its claws dug deep into her skin as it lifted her up by the front of her shirt. And in the next instant, Nioli was gone, carried away to a far corner of the castle grounds. It took several minutes for the child's screams to fade into silence. By that point, it was too late to stop her. The Beast continued to stalk after her, dragging her friend's body into the trees. The young prince cursed loudly under his breath. It was clear by the size of his pursuer that there were more than enough animals to feed themselves, so it wouldn't have mattered to the creature if there was one more. But the fact remained that the young man still hadn't seen any sign of Nioli, which meant that she was likely dead. He knew that, in most cases, if you didn't leave your victim alone, they usually died rather painfully. But it still bothered him. Despite the many times the Beast had hunted down people and left their corpses to rot in the woods, he couldn't bear the thought of watching that poor little girl die. So he spurred his horse into a gallop until he was out of sight. He paused beside the pond at the center of the kingdom to catch his breath, pulling his helmet off and running his hand through his hair. The sweat glistened off his brow and dripped down his nose, stinging his eyes. His clothes were covered in a thin layer of dust, making it seem like he'd been chasing her for days instead of hours. The young King sighed, wiping his forehead. After spending nearly two full years training to become a knight and having his skills honed during the short training camps where no amount of food or sleep would save him, he still had never seen nor fought anything like that before. Who knows what might have happened if she hadn't stumbled across the creature on her own? What kind of monster attacks children? The King pushed the thoughts out of his mind, pushing down the anger rising within his soul. He knew that Nioli's disappearance had nothing to do with the Beast. No, the Beast had simply appeared out of nowhere. The King's attention shifted to the body lying beneath the willow branches. He stared at the mangled remains, feeling his blood run cold at the sight of those horrible, jagged teeth biting into her soft, porcelain skin and tearing it away. The girl had probably done something foolish and reckless. Probably thought she could fight back by herself. Something had gone horribly wrong, and he wished she would hurry up and return. Maybe then the danger would all finally be over. A sudden movement drew his gaze to the other side of the pond. There, in a clearing amongst the trees, were three creatures. Three beasts with glowing white eyes and black fur snarling and growling at each other. They moved slowly and gracefully along the forest floor, avoiding stray leaves and twigs and the few small patches of snow on the ground. Their ears perked, and their tails began swishing back and forth, alerting the King that they had noticed his presence. One of them lunged at him, and the King quickly darted backward. Before he could regain his composure, the creature struck again, aiming for his leg. It caught his armor between two sharp claws and tore at it violently, causing him to fall to the ground. As he crawled backward, he held tight onto a loose piece of armor, which had come away from his thigh when he'd fallen. He quickly wrapped the piece of cloth around his wounded limb, which was dripping in blood. One of the beasts pounced on him again, but the King rolled out of its path easily this time. As the Beast landed back on the ground, another one launched itself at him as well, but the King jumped backward once more before it collided with him. Just as it reached the water's edge, he kicked it aside and leaped to his feet, glaring daggers at the Beast as it slowly made its way over to him. Another one leaped at him, but he swiftly dodged it. However, as soon as it landed on the ground, it immediately sprung back to life and charged at him again, ready to strike. The King's gaze locked on the Beast as he stepped sideways and kicked it in the chest, knocking it back to the forest floor and landing in the middle of the pond. He didn't bother giving it another look as he rushed past it and climbed out of the pond himself. By now, more animals had gathered around him. He ignored them as best as he could and kept walking, hoping to reach the town before dawn broke. The sun would rise earlier today due to the thick fog surrounding it that often covered the city in the early mornings. Despite that, a light always penetrated through it, shining brightly on the buildings surrounding the town. That light would allow him to better see his way through the city and avoid the numerous obstacles lying everywhere along the roads. However, he had crossed the bridge twice now, and he feared that the last time must have taken him much longer because he didn't even realize he was heading towards the center of town until it was too late. Now he had to navigate the crowded streets, hoping he wouldn't meet up with anyone from the village. As he passed the entrance to the main square, he spotted a woman carrying groceries in both hands as she walked down the sidewalk with the basket dangling dangerously close to falling apart. His eyes followed the line of her arms up, eventually catching her gaze. "Sorry," he apologized hurriedly, quickly averting his eyes from hers. "I don't want to interrupt, but do you happen to know how to go to the castle?" "Yes, I can show you where it is." "Thank you. Thank you so much." Before she could reply, however, a voice came from behind him. "Oh, hello again," said an unfamiliar female voice, accompanied by birds chirping. "Can I help you find something?" When he turned around, Nioli found herself face-to-face with none other than Eryn, the princess of Solaria. It wasn't uncommon for travelers to stop and buy some provisions from the local butcher for traveling merchants. Usually, there were plenty of vegetables and fruits and meat of all kinds laid out in large baskets. But this time, a couple of men, presumably the ones who had bought the goods, had piled them together and carried them off into the distance while a group of women followed closely behind. "Um, yes, actually." "Well, let me help you." Eryn placed a basket on the ground and crouched down. Without hesitation, Nioli handed the girl the sack of silver pieces the guards had given him. She nodded and carefully counted out seven of them before placing them inside the bag. She closed it and looked back up at the boy who stood next to her. "Are you looking for something particular?" she asked, holding the bag out towards him. "I'm sure I could tell you where exactly you need to go." He shook his head in response and smiled at her warmly. "No thanks. Just wanted to get these back to their owner." The girl frowned, looking confused, and stared at the coin bag for a moment before nodding, deciding not to ask further questions about it. "Okay. Well, good luck. And may the gods protect you." "Thanks." Nioli watched as Eryn started to walk away before turning around and following her. He hadn't planned on stopping anywhere else today, but he also didn't want to risk losing track of the princess and going in circles looking for her. But just as he stepped out of the door to enter the palace, Eryn stopped in place. When the boy glanced over at her, he noticed she was staring intently at something behind him. Turning around, he saw that she was gazing at the sky with a look of wonderment on her face. He followed her gaze upwards and noticed for the first time that the clouds were starting to part to let sunlight seep through. He squinted as he tried to determine where the light was coming from. As far as he knew, it was nighttime right now. "What are you looking at?" he wondered aloud. "It looks beautiful up there. Don't you think so?" He was surprised to find that her eyes were wet with tears. It seemed that this girl hadn't been crying recently. At least, he hadn't noticed any tears. Although it had been a while since he'd seen any signs of tears on her face, he didn't feel like taking any chances at the moment. "Let's go," he suddenly said, moving closer to the door. "There's still quite sometime before sunrise." With that, he left Eryn alone in the doorway to stare at the clouds. It was strange, he thought, but he couldn't say for sure if he had ever heard her call for her dog before. Perhaps she was trying to get her lost pet's attention. Or maybe her parents' dog. Perhaps a family dog was living around here, and she thought he might be nearby. Either way, he decided to take care of whatever problems she might have with her dog later. For now, it was time to put some money into her purse. After paying off the guard and making his way back up the steps leading to the tower, he quickly made his way into his room, closing the door behind him and quickly locking it. He didn't waste any time. He dropped his pack to the ground, unzipped the top pouch, pulled out the small box, and sat down on his bed, staring straight ahead. He opened the lid and gazed down upon the contents. The gold coins lay before him, sparkling in the early morning light streaming through the small window. A frown marred his features, and for a moment, he felt tempted to just throw the box to the ground and forget about finding a cure. He was tired of wasting all of the money he's made that he could spend on his medicine; after all, this was his chance to finally become rich. Even if he made a lot of money selling medicinal items to villagers during festivals or spring fairs, he felt he owed it all to his father. After all, he would never be able to repay the debt he owed the King for taking care of him his entire life. He needed to repay the man who raised him, who gave birth to him, and who loved him. And the only way to do that was to provide the man and his kingdom an heir, someone who would inherit what little wealth the King of Thieves could spare. Unfortunately, his father would never approve of his intentions, so he knew there was no way to fulfill them without getting the approval of the old King, and he doubted that he would ever agree to this kind of request. So why should he? What could he possibly gain from doing such things, anyway? He never understood the fascination of the noble ladies that surrounded him. They always told themselves that they loved being the queen, but he had witnessed many of their maidservants acting the same way when their lord and master were away. They would all obey him unconditionally if he were a king, yet he couldn't even bring himself to trust the servants who followed him around the palace. No matter how much he tried, he just couldn't understand it. For years, whenever a new prince or princess appeared, his parents insisted on that. They stay a few months in one city or another before returning home to the castle to rule alongside him. This served as another example of how ridiculous such a thing was, for the prince or princess had only spent one summer there. The fact remained that most of them either never married a single day in their lives, lived a miserable life, and eventually died young and without heirs. And that included the King and queen. All of their children, except their son, died in infancy; thus, their legacy had reached its peak, with only four remaining descendants. And if they managed to produce a child out of wedlock, they would marry that child to a commoner and pass their inheritance onto him. Not wanting to be considered a bastard himself, the young prince took great pains to avoid such an arrangement by staying at court, working hard, and avoiding every marriageable girl brought to the castle. So he was perfectly aware that he had never succeeded in meeting any of them either. Yet still, he didn't want to believe that his mother had simply forgotten about him and would probably never think about marrying again. Maybe he just hoped too much, or perhaps that was what his father would do, and try to keep a hold on him until the last possible minute, but to convince himself that this wouldn't turn out to be accurate, he needed more proof of their relationship than he already had. He took one deep breath in and exhaled slowly. He still couldn't figure out a solution, and it frustrated him to no end. To solve this problem, he needed to talk to the King. To convince him to send for an envoy. Because he hated the idea of marrying a woman he didn't even truly know, he couldn't imagine giving up the chance to see her again, especially as soon as he got to talk to the King alone. That was what he had come here for, after all. But how could he ask him to do that? Especially when the man had been so adamant and stubborn, to begin with. What could he possibly offer to persuade him to leave the throne behind for a mere stranger? He knew that it was impossible. Nothing would change his father's mind. Nothing. Suddenly, the sound of the heavy wooden door opening sounded behind him. Immediately, he jumped to his feet and turned around, facing Eryn, whose hair was still slightly damp from washing it. "You're done?" she asked, frowning slightly as she stared at him. He nodded. He had finished cleaning her hair almost five minutes ago. "How is your leg?" he questioned. She shrugged. "Fine. I'll live." He sighed softly to himself and shook his head. Despite his efforts to ignore it, the wound on her leg still hurt, and the bandage around it seemed to slowly fall off. "Come on then." He gestured for her to walk past him towards the large window that overlooked the gardens below. "We should find some food or drink for you before we return to the carriage." She nodded silently and walked across the room, sitting gingerly on the edge of her bed and leaning forward to rest her elbows on her knees. The blonde-haired boy turned his back to her and picked up the empty pack that rested against his foot. Opening it, he quickly removed the sack of coins he had stuffed inside earlier and placed it on the floor next to his bed, along with some dried fruit, water, and a couple of dried meat strips. Then, he pulled his cloak back on, grabbed the pack by the handle, and headed down the stairs. As he walked out of the room, he saw Eryn watching him from her chair at the bottom of the stairway. She was staring at him, seemingly waiting for something. Whatever she was waiting for, he had no clue what. It seemed like she had forgotten about the whole business of the gold coins he'd paid off that guard moments ago. She smiled lightly at him and then looked away, not saying anything. "Where are we going?" When he didn't reply, she furrowed her eyebrows slightly. "Do you want me to follow you?" she repeated. "I can carry your bag." Once more, he didn't respond. "If you don't tell me where you're going, I won't be able to follow." She was getting impatient. She couldn't wait any longer. He kept silent and looked forward, continuing to walk down the winding hallway until reaching a set of doors. He stopped in front of a dark grey door and unlocked it with a key hanging around his neck. With one quick tug, he opened the door, allowing the light streaming through from above to spill onto the floor, revealing a staircase that led downwards. As he descended the steps, he heard Eryn following close behind. Her footsteps rang loudly against the wooden floors as her dress swished back and forth slightly. He glanced over at her briefly and watched as she lowered her head slightly, her eyes fixed squarely on the ground before her. They entered a wide corridor stretched out in both directions until it ended at a pair of massive doors that stood at the very end. Standing outside the doors was a guard resting his hands on his sword hilts as he peered down menacingly at the two visitors approaching him. The young boy stopped, turned around, and faced Eryn, who also came to a halt several paces behind him. The boy pointed towards one of the doors without saying anything, and together they padded to it. The guard continued to watch them as they passed underneath him. Once they had closed the door behind themselves, they stopped moving and listened to what might be beyond those doors. They heard nothing. There was silence. They both moved further into the room until they had disappeared entirely from view, leaving only the faintest trace of their presence behind to show their trail had ever existed in the first place. Then, after turning around to face each other again, they hurried through the room and ran out of the door and through the hall. Finally, they stopped in front of one of the doors, looking at one another with concern. Neither of them spoke a word. For a few seconds, neither said anything until finally, the young lad broke the silence. "It's locked," he whispered in surprise. "The guards must have taken care of that." The young lady's brows were raised in confusion. "Why would they lock it?" she asked, staring at the door in confusion and suspicion. His blue eyes flickered between the wooden doors in front of them. "Because of something inside, I presume," he guessed, glancing around them in search of something that could lead them to the correct answer. But nothing was within his reach. His hands began feeling hot under his gloves, but he ignored them and started pulling his sleeves upwards, trying to remove them. But before he could take them off, the doors suddenly opened, causing them both to jump backward in fright. Two men stepped out of the gate, wearing black uniforms and swords at their side. They walked straight to the middle of the hallway without speaking and crossed their arms, blocking their path. Both boys froze in shock at the sight of them. One of them was taller than the other, and his long blonde hair cascaded down to cover half of his face. He wore a mask that covered everything but his mouth and nose. His eyes were covered with golden plates that protected them from seeing the person beneath the disguise. In addition to that, his entire body had been enveloped in flames. The boy beside him did the same with his own hoodie and a thick black cloak, while his partner remained motionless, with one hand pressed tightly against his chest, hiding the wound there. A few inches shorter than the blond youth, his companion looked even younger, though his skin was as pale as snow. Unlike his partner, who held a flame in one hand and had a sword strapped across his shoulder, he carried no weapon. His long blond locks hung to his waist, and his green eyes sparkled brightly as if reflecting the fire burning inside him. Then, as the boy realized what had happened, he swallowed loudly and stared at the two warriors with a mixture of fear, awe, anger, disgust, and contempt. He didn't understand why these people felt the need to confront him like that. After being given a choice to join the war effort, he hadn't wanted to enlist and made sure to make everyone aware of that. Why were these men, who looked relatively harmless, suddenly doing this? Was this really what they expected him to say? Finally, the blond youth spoke. "Who are you?" he shouted in anger. No response. "Who sent you?" he added. No response. "Answer us! Who are you?!" No reply. "Tell me!" Still no response. He clenched his fists angrily and glared back and forth between the two warriors. "Why are you doing this? Tell me what you want from me!" Silence. "Speak up, damn you!" he shouted. "What do you want from me?" A sudden blast of fire erupted from the palm of one of the warriors, causing both boys to flinch and shield their faces with their hands. "What are you doing?!" the blond screamed in terror, raising his voice even higher, his eyes growing wider as he gazed at the flames dancing wildly in the direction from which the attack had come. After a momentary pause, the fire gradually dissipated, and the young man's face regained its calm expression. He took a step back from the young boy, bowed slightly towards him, and reached over and pushed open the other door. Stepping inside, the two men immediately disappeared from view, the doors shutting swiftly behind them, just as another blast of fire exploded from the man's palm and rushed down towards the blond teenager with a roar. Just as he prepared to scream, he instinctively dropped to his knees as the heat of the flames hit him full force, causing him to cry out in pain. His vision clouded over as tears welled up in his eyes, threatening to flood out of his eyes. The boy fell to his right side and curled into a ball, his arms wrapped protectively around his torso. Suddenly, he felt warm lips pressing gently against his forehead as a familiar scent wafted past his nostrils; Eryn kissed him tenderly on the top of his head. He lifted his head weakly and looked up at her, blinking as the tears spilled slowly down his cheeks. Then, he leaned over, put his right arm around her waist, and hugged her gently, burying his face in her chest. She wrapped her arms tightly around his shoulders and kissed the top of his head again. Eryn The next morning dawned bright and clear, as usual. Eryn rose early every day, just like she had every morning since arriving in Capital, and she spent most of the day either training or reading, taking advantage of the many books that had been brought into the room with her the night before. When the sun had barely risen enough that it shone into the room, Eryn rose to her feet and quickly dressed in a simple blue dress, tying her blonde tresses into a loose ponytail at the back of her head with an elastic band. She took her satchel, slipped her dagger back into the scabbard on her belt, and grabbed her sword and shield before heading out of the room. She exited the room, softly closing the door behind her so she wouldn't wake anyone up. Once she arrived in the dining hall, she noticed the tables were already filled with people talking amongst themselves. Everyone's attention immediately shifted to her as soon as she arrived. Her eyebrows knitted slightly as she glanced around at everyone, unaware of the big deal. She shrugged her shoulders when she realized how silly she probably looked. She approached one of the free tables and sat down. The chatter instantly died away. The table's occupants seemed to study her carefully as if deciding whether or not to speak with her. Finally, the woman closest to her cleared her throat and addressed her. "You must be Eryn. We've been expecting you," she said calmly. "Do you know why you're here? Or why it's necessary to meet in a room like this?" "I'm here because I'm sick of being treated like a prisoner," she answered coldly. "That is understandable, but we can help you get better if you give us a chance to explain ourselves." She sighed and leaned back in her seat. "Fine. Explain yourself. If you make this quick, I'll leave this place without further problems." "Very well. My name is Amalia, and I am your personal healer. I work for the King himself, and I am in charge of making sure you all recover from your sickness and get rid of it properly," she said calmly as she took a sip of her soup. "My job is straightforward and consists mainly of treating your illness's symptoms and ensuring your body gets the rest that it needs." "So, basically, what you mean by this whole thing is that I should stay here until I'm healthy again?" "Yes. Your condition is not contagious." Eryn nodded as she thought about this, letting her mind wander slightly as she tried to find an explanation for what she was going to do. It wasn't until several minutes later that she finally realized exactly what she would do. She looked directly at Amalia and smiled brightly. "Thank you for explaining all of this, Dr. Amalia. I am grateful for this chance to get away. If you don't mind, I will begin by finishing my meal. You will probably want to return to your quarters and continue preparing whatever it is you've prepared for me to eat so I can start getting better sooner."

Amalia smiled. "Of course. I'll see you tomorrow." Once Amalia left the room, Eryn went back to eating her soup quietly, observing her surroundings. As soon as she was finished, she got up and headed towards the exit, grabbing her satchel once more as she did so. As she walked through the halls, she passed several other children who looked just like her, all staring curiously at her. They all seemed interested in what she was doing, but none approached her. She continued walking down the path until she reached the outside gate and headed for her horse. Once she stood next to him, she grabbed his reins and pulled herself onto his back, securing her hold. He began to saunter towards the entrance where he would usually wait but stopped when a large crowd appeared in front of them. Everyone gathered around and blocked their way, staring at Eryn with varied expressions, curiosity, confusion, and hostility. "Hello there, Eryn. Did you sleep well last night?" asked one woman whose face was obscured by her blonde, curly hair. "Oh yes, thank you, it was fine," she responded. "Are you ready for breakfast? You look pretty pale, are you alright?" said another woman. "Hey! Don't try to trick her, you idiot; she's obviously not sick," yelled yet another girl. Eryn ignored everything else the women were saying, focusing her gaze ahead while holding the mare's reins firmly. More than twenty were blocking the way and surrounding her, all appearing angry and confused. But as they talked among themselves, some of them laughed and shook their heads and muttered to each other, apparently arguing whether it was wise to let her pass. "It seems to me she isn't afraid to ride her horse in front of all of you like a common criminal!" shouted one of them. "Is that true, Eryn?" Eryn lowered her head and tightened her grip on the bridle. This caused her mare to move forward, almost bumping into several people. A few other horses started neighing and snorting, causing everyone else to move aside and let the two animals go. At first, the two horses galloped slowly through the crowd, but a moment later, Eryn found herself riding alongside the others standing in front of the gates. Before she had gone very far, though, she heard the sound of a trumpet blaring somewhere in the distance. The trumpet seemed incredibly close, and although she could not hear the noise, she realized that it came from inside the Capital and knew instinctively that it was coming from the Temple of Life itself. The loud booming sound echoed throughout the city, and the city's citizens were all startled, looking anxiously toward the source of the sound. A few moments later, the sounds grew louder, causing the ground to tremble vigorously underneath their feet. The people gasped in shock as they saw the massive army of monsters in the vast forest. Some monsters were bigger than mountains, some larger than houses, and covered in white fur. Many creatures were also seen emerging from the trees with spears pointed directly at the army as if they had set out to kill those on the spot. "Aaaaaah!" cried someone as a group of monsters charged toward a small group of soldiers. "They're the Beast Clan! Run!" screamed a child as the monsters' huge claws ripped apart the soldiers' armor. As the soldiers fought bravely to defend themselves, a small squad of soldiers suddenly emerged from the bushes and charged straight at the Beasts. One of the monsters roared as it turned toward the approaching soldiers, swiping with its sharp claws towards one of them. A soldier managed to duck beneath the monster's paw before shooting arrows at it, striking it straight in the shoulder. The Beast roared angrily, glaring at the soldier who had injured it, who shot arrows at it again, only to miss. However, the Beast wasn't having any of it. It quickly raised its other arm and struck the arrow out of the air. The soldier cried out in pain as he fell to the ground, clutching his right leg and screaming loudly. Eryn clenched her teeth, clenching both hands on the reigns tightly. As the Beast lifted his paw, ready to strike, Eryn kicked her horse hard against the side of his stomach and urged him into motion, leaving him momentarily stunned. Just as quickly, the creature recovered from his surprise and began swinging his heavy tail back and forth, knocking soldiers off their feet and causing them to tumble. More arrows flew towards him and pierced their flesh, causing the soldiers to scream and cry out in pain. Eryn jumped out of the saddle before he fully stopped moving, pulling her sword from its sheath and swinging it at the Beast with great force. The blade sliced through thick skin with ease and embedded deep into the Beast's neck, effectively killing it, but she felt no satisfaction over such an easy victory. After all, the soldier had still managed to injure the Beast before she arrived and had been unable to kill it. Instead of feeling relieved that she'd killed the Beast, she merely felt disappointed that she hadn't been able to protect any of the innocent soldiers trying their best to keep the beasts at bay. The Beast roared loudly before collapsing and falling to the earth, twitching violently before dying in seconds. With nothing left to do but stand and stare at it, Eryn stared blankly at the body until she noticed someone behind her. She turned her eyes to the woman who was looking at her curiously. "What happened? Why did you kill it?" she asked with genuine curiosity. Eryn shrugged casually as if she didn't care at all what had happened. "I don't know. Maybe it was stupid to attack it, and maybe not," she replied, ignoring the other woman. Her answer was short and abrupt enough to catch the other woman off guard, and her eyebrows rose skeptically. "Well, I don't think it was stupid," she argued. Eryn shrugged and began heading towards the road again. "No offense taken, I suppose, but you don't really seem to care much what I think about your decisions," she stated plainly as she rode past Amalia. Without waiting for a response from the doctor, Eryn continued down the road that led into the city. After several hours of riding on the streets, Eryn finally arrived at the edge of the town and dismounted from her horse, and walked briskly toward the Temple entrance. "Where are you going?" yelled a voice behind her before stopping her in her tracks. She looked around, searching for the source of the sound as she slowly took slow and cautious steps. "Don't turn around, or you might hurt yourself," said another voice behind her. Eryn stopped turning and looked back. Two young men were standing where her horse had come to a complete stop in the middle of the street. Both were armed to the teeth, one holding a crossbow and the other carrying a pair of swords. One of the men held a knife in his hands while the other had a long spear, looking at her curiously. Although she couldn't see their faces clearly from a distance, she figured they must be members of the royal guards. She then wondered why they were talking with her instead of protecting her. "So, how come you didn't run away when you saw all of us here? We could have killed you in a second without you even realizing anything was wrong with you," inquired the man holding the spear. The man with the crossbow aimed his weapon right at her heart, which sent chills running down her spine as she watched his finger tighten over the trigger. She knew that should he pull the trigger, she wouldn't be able to escape in time. In fact, she would likely die immediately. Nevertheless, she remained silent. "You're a coward! You know exactly why we aren't chasing you. And you don't want to find out what happens if you don't follow our orders correctly, do you?" he demanded threateningly. She refused to give them an answer, so they decided to take action instead. They charged at her simultaneously with a battle cry, weapons raised and ran straight at her. She was still alive today because she had been quick enough to react and dodge the first wave of attack. However, the second wave caught her completely by surprise. She tried to escape the onslaught, only to have three soldiers rush up behind her and grab hold of her wrists. Before she could do anything, they dragged her backward until she was forced to sit down on her legs at the edge of the road and helplessly watch as they surrounded her. She wanted to protest to her captors, to beg them to release her, but fear overwhelmed every other part of her system. If they could overpower her physically, what chance did she have against four skilled warriors? However, her attempts at fighting back ended up futile, as the three soldiers grabbed hold of her arms and legs, tied them together with rope, and dragged her down the road. She attempted to break free from their grip repeatedly but failed. By the time she reached the palace, her arms, thighs, and calves were bruised, and she was covered in blood. Although there were several bruises all along her arms and legs, the worst was the cuts that cut open the skin on the backs of her legs and ankles, causing the blood to seep out profusely. Although she had several cuts across her face and hands, they weren't nearly as bad as they appeared. When the soldiers finally placed her in the dungeon, they chained her to the wall. The jail was filled with hundreds of cages containing prisoners that she recognized: Children from the village. None looked healthy, nor had they grown well since she had last visited the prison. Their hair was thin, their bodies were scrawny, and most had become sick from malnutrition. Some of the children even looked quite frail, but it was easy to tell that they were solid and healthy, as evidenced by the fact that none of them had died despite all their hardships. When Eryn was locked in, she could barely move her feet and hands, even though they'd been securely shackled to the wall. Once the door to the dungeon was closed and locked, the guards departed the room, leaving only Eryn and another prisoner to share it. As they sat side by side, staring at each other as if sizing up the other person, Eryn couldn't help but ask him what had happened to him and how many people had been murdered by the Beasts. After hearing that the other prisoner was from the town where she lived, he told her everything that had happened. He also informed her of what had happened between him and some villagers earlier. The villagers, who were the ones who had attacked the villagers, were a band of rebels. The other prisoner said that they'd attacked them while they had been celebrating a successful harvest. As far as the prisoner knew, they were the soldiers of the Emperor. Had killed many people and stole their money. That, he believed, had prompted them to attack the village in the first place. For now, neither the prisoner nor anyone else seemed to care about what had happened. They had nearly succeeded in destroying the village, as they all seemed content with just staying inside the dungeons of the prison. The prisoner explained to her that he, like her, was a prisoner just like everyone else in this jail. No matter how hard Eryn fought them, they were stronger than she was, making it almost impossible for her to get free. Eryn then realized that she was alone, and although it saddened her greatly, she eventually fell asleep and dreamed of nothing. Eryn woke up the following day to the sound of someone knocking on the bars of her cell and yelling to let her out, and it was clear she wasn't getting out any time soon. As she opened her eyes, she found herself face to face with two large dogs that had been watching her sleep. They snarled as they growled, baring their small, sharp teeth and fangs at her menacingly. She gulped nervously and shuddered slightly, terrified that these monsters were close to her. Slowly backing away from the cage, she moved to the opposite end of the room and curled up in a corner, sitting on her knees and leaning against the wall with her back against the cold stone, shaking uncontrollably as she listened to the dog's howl and snarl. When the dogs' angry yells subsided slightly, she dared to glance at the cages again and noticed that one of the larger dogs had gotten bored with playing with her and was lying down, his head resting atop its paws as he yawned. At the same time, its partner continued pacing around the small confines of its cage. After a few moments to calm her breathing, Eryn slowly stood up and moved toward the smaller cage. Once she got closer to the smaller one, she paused and glanced back at the large dog. The animal had fallen asleep, its tail lazily wagging behind it, oblivious to her presence.

Hesitantly approaching the large dog, Eryn reached through the cage bars to pet its head. It jumped slightly when she touched its fur but ignored her as it continued to lie peacefully beside itself. After calming herself, Eryn stepped out of the cage and turned to inspect the other cells, trying to determine who was who and whether they were friendly. All her previous friends had either died or left dead, but she had managed to survive the massacre and escape from captivity, so hopefully, she could make it through this too. After examining the cages for a few more minutes, she headed to the large cage door and gently pushed it open. It creaked a little under her weight, but it wasn't loud enough to alert the beasts inside the cages. Walking over to the large enclosure, she carefully climbed onto the platform above the cell. She crouched on the metal platform and looked down at her friend. "Hello, Arlin," greeted Eryn, smiling softly at him. He smiled back up at her and licked the top of her hand. A few minutes later, Eryn heard the sounds of chains rattling coming from somewhere behind her. Turning cautiously, she spotted her father's sword propped against the wall beside the door. She quickly grabbed and swung it forward, narrowly missing the wolf's throat that had crept up behind her. Just as the wolf lunged at her, her father jumped off a wooden beam and came into view. Without saying anything, he drew a dagger from his belt, plunged it into the chest of the wolf attacking her, and sliced off its head. Then he tossed the bloody blade aside and approached her, pulling her up and hugging her tightly. "I'm sorry I couldn't protect you," murmured Eryn before she started weeping. She'd never seen her father so distraught. "Are you alright?" Her father released her. "It looks like you've been in quite a fight." His eyebrows were knitted together as he examined her body, looking for any signs of injury or cuts. After finding nothing, he pulled her towards him. "Let's go home." Home. It was nice to hear that term again after everything that had transpired between her and her father, although she knew that there were still plenty of enemies. However, that didn't matter right now. Right now, her main priority should be to take care of her injured arm and see if she could use her magic to heal herself. Once they returned home, he would teach her about healing spells and how best to use them. With his guidance guiding her actions, she managed to recover her mana without much trouble, although the wounds caused by the wounds from the wolf's attacks hurt a lot, especially her left wrist, which had been cut open during that incident. Once she healed her wound completely, she took her arm and wrapped it with gauze and bandages before placing her arm on the ground in front of her. A blue flame ignited from within her palm, and she focused on controlling the fire. She then raised her hand high and shouted a powerful spell word with as much power behind it as she could muster. In an instant, thousands of tiny stars and constellations were shot out. Her palm spread across the sky. After she had finished, she lowered her hand and stared at it in awe before she collapsed onto her back. Even though she was exhausted, she couldn't help but smile from the excitement of having done such a fantastic feat. When her mother heard that her daughter was safe and had survived the battle, she immediately burst into tears, not caring that her husband was watching her from afar. She rushed towards her son and embraced him fiercely, unable to believe that Eryn was finally back with her. As her son returned the hug, holding her tightly in his arms, Eryn watched as her parents rejoiced for several minutes before finally releasing each other. The celebration continued throughout the night as Eryn and her father recounted everything that had happened in their escape from the palace. While her parents listened patiently to what Eryn had to say, her husband did not take the news as well as her father did. Her father, after telling them everything that had happened in the palace and the battle they'd witnessed in the mountains, explained to her husband everything that he and Eryn had accomplished over the past year, including the events leading up to them escaping. The King listened intently until her father had finished speaking before he responded. "You saved my life," the King stated, turning to look at his wife, who was now sitting next to him on the floor, gazing lovingly at her beautiful baby girl. "And I will always be grateful to you for helping me find her, for helping us survive." Reaching up, he caressed her cheek, causing her to giggle quietly. "We're lucky that we are alive; I can't imagine what the punishment may have been if your father hadn't found us." "Yes," replied Eryn with a sigh, "I'm very thankful for him rescuing us, and I hope he won't have any problems finding us. But even luck can run out sooner or later. You know, we really shouldn't depend on luck; sometimes, you need help from others, especially since we don't even know where our enemy is." Once the celebrations had ended and most of the prisoners had returned to their respective cells, the two kings decided to talk about what had happened earlier in the day and what they would do next. Eryn explained that her father had told her to stay in the village because it was safe. The townspeople had helped them when they arrived, but once she had discovered who the attackers were and who they belonged to, it was only natural for her to leave. Although she wanted to accompany her father, her mother reminded her that he wouldn't have wanted her to endanger herself unnecessarily and that she had to stay in the village. Her father insisted that, although she had been brave enough to travel on foot through the snow to his castle, he wouldn't forgive himself if something happened to her while she traveled through the forest alone. So, after convincing her father that she needed to remain in the village, she and her mother left for the Capital. Although she wished she could've been there with her parents to protect them, Eryn decided to wait for another opportunity. After her conversation with her mother, Eryn chose to return to her room and check on Arlin. As soon as she entered the room and saw that he was still sleeping peacefully, she sighed in relief and sat down next to him on the bed. She tenderly stroked the fur on his face, ensuring he was okay before falling asleep next to him. The following day Eryn woke up feeling somewhat lightheaded due to sleep deprivation. She slowly opened her eyes and groaned loudly when she realized that she must've passed out in bed sometime last night. Feeling incredibly thirsty, she reached over to the side table for her glass of water to drink but instead of finding it empty, she accidentally knocked over Arlin's bowl, which sent its contents flying everywhere. Quickly getting up and retrieving the bowl from the ground, she placed it on the table and filled it up before carrying it over to the bed to put on the nightstand. After cleaning Arlin's mess up and setting the bowl back on the table, she went to the wardrobe to search for a pair of trousers to wash off the dirt and grime on her body from yesterday's adventure. When she had gotten dressed, she noticed that the basket containing her dinner had been moved to the room's window, revealing the small amount of sunlight that seeped through the curtains. She walked over and picked up the basket before heading towards the window to eat her meal. After finishing her food and washing the dish using the pitcher provided, she set it down on the tray and went downstairs to get some breakfast. Her mother was already seated at the breakfast table, eating her own breakfast. As soon as she noticed Eryn entering, she stood up from her chair and came over to greet her daughter with a smile. Eryn hugged her mother, but as she began to pull away, she stopped and asked, "Mum, what time is it?" "Well, it's early, but judging by the fact that you came down so quickly, I assume that it isn't that late yet. Why? Do you want to go back upstairs? Do you wish to rest more?" Eryn shook her head and replied, "No, Mum. I just want to know how long it will be until my birthday is up, that's all." With a worried look on her face, Eryn's mother answered, "Your My birthday is in five days, sweetheart. Are you sure that you don't want to rest first? If you need to take a break and relax, that's fine too." "No, mum. I'm fine. We haven't gotten any gifts for my birthday since we returned to the kingdom, so I guess that's why. Can't I go up and grab the gift for my birthday?" She smiled hopefully at her mother, wanting to spend a few hours with her, enjoying her company. Her mother thought about it for a second, biting her lower lip as she tried to decide whether she felt comfortable letting her daughter roam around the castle unescorted since she was still recovering, especially from her injury, but eventually, she agreed. "Okay, sweetheart. You may go up and grab the present for your birthday," said the queen. After seeing the look on Eryn's face change slightly at the mention of her presents, she hurried to add, "Just give me a minute to finish packing up some things for tomorrow. Go ahead and go up, and I'll join you shortly." The queen nodded before rushing towards their bedroom and closing the door. A smile appeared on Eryn's lips as she left the kitchen and headed upstairs to get her present from her mother. She was excited to discover who gave her this beautiful bracelet she wore every day of her life.